Alaric's

Alaric's Bow:
A Book of the Amari
By
KateMarie Collins

Alaric's Bow: A Book of the Amari

ALL RIGHTS RESERVED

No part of this book may be reproduced or transmitted in any form or by any means, electronic or mechanical, including photocopying, recording, or by any information storage and retrieval system, without permission in writing from the author, except in the case of brief quotations embodied in reviews.

Cover Art:
Michelle Crocker
www.mlcdesigns4you.com

Publisher's Note:

This is a work of fiction. All names, characters, places, and events are the work of the author's imagination.

Any resemblance to real persons, places, or events is coincidental.

Solstice Publishing -
www.solsticepublishing.com

Copyright 2015 KateMarie Collins

Alaric's Bow: A Book of the Amari

For the Archers of

The Barony of Glymm Mere.

May their aim ever be true.

Alaric's Bow: A Book of the Amari

Alaric's Bow: A Book of the Amari

Chapter One

Kai crouched behind the ferns and rocks, waiting. He'd been there since dawn. His legs no longer ached. They waited, like the rest of him.

At last, his patience rewarded him. A small rustle moved across the forest floor, carried on the breeze blowing toward him. The boar came into view. Kai's hand deftly notched the arrow he'd held loosely against the bow. Drawing back, he took aim. Today, he would be the one bringing home the prize for the feast. Not his brother.

The arrow flew through the air, plunging into the boar's side. It toppled over, dead. Kai stood, slinging his bow over his shoulder. He placed one hand on the rock in front of him, preparing to climb over it toward his kill. The clapping behind him halted his movement.

"Well shot, little one!" A deep voice dripped with sarcasm. "You managed to make it so we can go celebrate instead of staying out here for hours."

Alaric's Bow: A Book of the Amari

Kai turned. His older brother stood there, surrounded by his cronies. "I killed it, Kaerdan. That's not yours."

Kaerdan stepped forward. "It doesn't matter, does it? Because they'll all say it was mine." With one hand, he gestured at his cronies swarming the dead animal. Ruffling Kai's brown hair as he walked past him, he laughed. "Grow up, brother. There's nothing you can do to prove otherwise. You're the spare. I'm the heir. You're just a backup in case something happened to me as a child. Father never intended for you to take the throne. He never has. He couldn't even give you a proper name."

"Our mother named me, same as you," Kai called after his brother. All Kaerdan did to acknowledge his words was a rude gesture as he went to see "his" trophy.

Sighing resolutely, Kai took his time to gather his pack and make the walk back to the keep. He should've known better. All his life, his brother had taken credit for things Kai had done. Laid claim to things he liked. Reminded him, at every chance, that he was the lesser son.

Their parents didn't fight for him whenever he pressed his case. Respect your

Alaric's Bow: A Book of the Amari

brother, for he will be King after your father. He will marry well—unite the residents of the island. Once that happened, they would be a force to be reckoned with. As long as the factions warred with each other, they couldn't regain what had been lost.

There wasn't much room for him once Kaerdan's marriage took place. Sure, Father would rule a few more years. Barring some accident or early death, that is. The earliest he would abdicate in favor of Kaerdan would be after he produced his own heir. And that was never certain.

He'd heard the stories from his mother. Of a land rich with resources. Farms and forests, cities and ports. His grandfather's court, where ladies wore beautiful jewels and men wore cloaks woven of pure silver. Where even the Amari wore chains studded with emeralds and rubies.

His mother filled his head with tales during his youth. She never said it, but he knew she missed the trappings of her father's palace. The bitterness that tinged her voice when she spoke of coming to the island and marrying her father wasn't well masked. Over time, she even stopped hiding it.

Alaric's Bow: A Book of the Amari

"If I could, I'd send you there, Kai. You'd be able to marry far more advantageously than you would here. What's left, after Kaerdan weds? That old fool that calls himself King to the North, Ian. He didn't have enough sense to father a son. No, just a daughter. And only one! How can you be expected to marry someone equal to us in station? There's barely any pure bloodlines left on this backward island!" Her contempt rang in his ears at the memory.

The bright sun reflected off the high stone walls of the main keep. Kai squinted against the glare as he emerged from the sheltering woods. He could see Kaerdan and his friends, shouting about how "great" the hunt was, crossing the far field. The Amari working the crops paused to give respect, but said nothing. It didn't surprise him. Many feared what would become of them when Father died. Almost as much as Kai wondered himself.

It didn't really matter, in the end. He knew he'd be leaving the island once Kaerdan wore the crown. His brother had made it very clear that he saw Kai as little more than an inconvenient brother. Five

Alaric's Bow: A Book of the Amari

years separated them. It might as well be fifteen for how big the gulf between them was.

He heard the tall grain to the left of the path rustle, knew the lightness of the step as Holly drew up beside him. Amari or not, she was a friend. One of the few people he'd miss when he left.

"I see the Prince has decided what is his is yours once again," she said.

Kai shrugged. "It doesn't matter. Let him have the glory. I'd rather choke on rotten meat than eat at table with him."

She laughed. "If it matters so little, why does it eat at you so much? At least you still have your freedom. You can come and go as you desire. You're of age now. Take your leave of your father and find your own way."

He stopped and turned to look at her. Resisting the urge to tuck a stray lock of brown hair back under her bonnet, he smiled at her. "And who would take care of you if I did? Maybe I should go to Father tonight, let him know I want you as my own." His grin faded as he saw the muscles in her face tense up.

"If that is your will, Prince." The title came out of her like a hiss. "What is it

Alaric's Bow: A Book of the Amari

to be Amari but to serve those who chain us?"

Reaching out a hand, he hesitated as he saw her draw back. "That's not what I meant and you know it. Amari or not, I'd take you with me as a friend. Nothing more. Not unless you asked."

Holly looked at him, the gold eyes aflame with anger and fear. "That's the problem, Prince. You are not the one who is chained and must obey." She bobbed a quick curtsey, "By your leave. I have duties I must attend to." Without another word, she dove back into the wheat field.

Kai's mood was still black as he entered the keep. Much as he liked Holly, he didn't understand her most days. The Amari here weren't treated badly. They had shelter; homes were kept warm and dry from the winter snows. They had work to keep them busy, clothing and shoes given to them. None went hungry. And it's not like Father demanded them to use magic often. Sure, it happened sometimes. But the wars were long over. Few bore the scars of what they'd been commanded to do. For the last sixteen years, there'd been peace. The pact joining a seven-year old Kaerdan to the newborn,

Alaric's Bow: A Book of the Amari

Jenny, when she reached eighteen was enough to keep things quiet.

He crossed the courtyard, not seeing the bustle about him. He just couldn't understand what Holly's problem was. It's not like he'd be a bad master to her. And it really was time for him to start establishing his own household. Second son or not, he was still a Prince. One that could travel with an entourage, have his own Amari. And one as gifted as Holly was would be an asset when he was looking for a bride.

A loud grumble from his stomach reminded him he'd left before breakfast. Rather than disturb anyone, he took a left at the next junction and headed down to the kitchens. Olive would be there, and she always had food for him.

The kitchens were a flurry of activity. Dozens of Amari darted about, intent on their duties. Few paid much attention to him as he entered, too focused on the tasks at hand. Kai stopped short before he collided with a pair of men hauling the boar he killed less than an hour earlier on a spit between them. He watched, curious, as they situated the iron rod on the notches above the huge cooking fire.

Alaric's Bow: A Book of the Amari

"Is someone coming?" he remarked to the room at large.

"Aye, Prince. Your brother's bride and her family sent word. The roads are good and they'll be here by the evening meal." Olive spoke, not looking up from the huge pile of dough she was kneading on the table in front of her. "We'll be celebrating a wedding in the morning."

Kai stepped back slightly, dodging another person as they hurried past with a bowl of fruit. "Tomorrow? Is it that soon?"

"Helen, get that bread in the oven right away!" Olive called out instructions better than a military commander. "Indeed it is. We thought we'd have another week or more to prepare. Watch the broth, Tobias! Burn that and you'll eat naught else for a week!"

Slowly, Kai retreated from the kitchen, grabbing a small meat pie from an unguarded bowl as he left. Had he remained, he would've been one more person in the way.

As he twisted his way through the stone corridors, he found himself dodging more and more people as they hurried about. Bunches of fragrant lavender and sage dotted the walls, chasing away the lingering mustiness of the castle. Clouds of dust could be seen rising in the air as tapestries were beaten clean. All to make a good first impression on the woman who would sit next to Kaerdan on the throne.

No longer caring, Kai retreated to the solitude of his chamber.

Alaric's Bow: A Book of the Amari

Chapter Two

Kai stuck to the shadows, avoiding the revelry of the wedding feast. A sense of dread had encompassed him since the arrival of the bridal party the day before. Something was wrong, but he couldn't put his finger on what.

Kaerdan and his new wife, Jenny, sat at the head table, their fathers flanking the happy couple. Her blonde hair shone in the candles illuminating the hall. Kaerdan did have a preference for fair-haired ladies. In that, he would be happy.

It was his mother, however, that drew his attention. She rarely left her rooms any more, claiming illness. Tonight, though, no sign of sickness decorated her pale face. If anything, it glowed in triumph. And why shouldn't it? Her firstborn married, ready to continue the family name. Soon, he would be King.

His father rose from his place, chalice in hand. "Today was a glorious day! A wedding, a new treaty, and a successful hunt! Kaerdan is truly gifted and his prize

Alaric's Bow: A Book of the Amari

sits radiant beside him. To the happy couple!"

Kai shifted through the people near him. Gifted, indeed. The only thing his brother had ever been able to do was take credit for someone else's deeds.

He needed air. The hall was nauseatingly sweet, between the overabundance of the beeswax candles to the boar—his kill—roasting on the spit. Winding his way through the drunk wedding guests, he made his way to the upper gallery. Outside would've been preferable, but he knew better. At some point, he'd be expected to go forward and pledge his loyalty to his father and brother. Not that the words meant anything to him. He stopped believing in the vow after seeing how little they meant to Kaerdan.

"Where's the Historian?" his father's voice boomed through the arched hallway. Kai smiled a little. The recitation of the family line would take a good deal of time. Tradition, yes. But it also gave him enough time to breathe some air not saturated with sweat, ale, and food.

"Kai," Holly whispered from a recessed doorway. "Do you trust me?"

Alaric's Bow: A Book of the Amari

He blinked at her, puzzled. "Of course. Why wouldn't I? It's not like you can lie to me." He flinched at the anger that flashed across her face. She didn't need the reminder of her status.

"You need to come with me. Now." Reaching out, she pulled at his hand. Her voice tumbled over the words.

In the back of his mind, he heard the Historian drone on. He was covering the family fast. The old Amari had been with them since he was an infant, and was tasked with remembering each birth and death. Every family on the island kept a Historian to prove noble birth.

"Holly, I can't. As soon as Old Josiah is done, I have to go down and make my pledge. If I miss that, Father will have my hide."

She licked her lips, her gold eyes darting past him. "Kai, there won't be any way around that. Once Josiah is finished, things are going to go bad for you. Quickly." She pulled on his hand once again. "Please, I beg you. Come with me now while you can still run." Her eyes welled up with tears.

"Run? What am I running from?"

The hall below became silent. Too silent. He heard his father's massive oak

Alaric's Bow: A Book of the Amari

chair slide across the floor. "Josiah, you forgot one of my sons. Why did you not add Kai to the list?"

Tearing his arm from Holly's grasp, Kai turned and looked down. Something knotted in his stomach. Whether it was fear or apprehension, he didn't know.

"I am Amari," the old man croaked. "I cannot lie. You asked for a recitation of the legitimate line. I have given you that."

Susana, his mother, spoke across the chamber. Her voice snapped with irritation and fear. "No, Josiah. Kai is true born. He should be on your list."

"Prince Kai is son of his Majesty, yes. But not by you, my Queen. He was begotten on an Amari brought over after a raid. You traded your own stillborn son to his mother so he might live. His only saving grace being his eyes were that of his father, not his mother. Kai is half Islander, half Amari."

The assembled guests broke out in a fury of voices. Kai staggered back against the wall, stunned. He was half Amari? Kaerdan'd have him in chains the moment he saw him.

Something pulled at his wrist, hard, insistent. He looked, afraid it was a guard.

Alaric's Bow: A Book of the Amari

Already he could hear his brother demanding both Kai's attendance and a blacksmith. Holly stood next to him, her face full of compassion. "Kai, please. We have to get you away from here, now. Before it's too late!"

Fear released him from his shock. Nodding, he followed her as she led him through a back staircase. The dust, thick on the walls, gave him a small sliver of hope they'd make it out. The few that came through here were servants. Kaerdan probably didn't know it even existed.

"We knew, the moment the message came about their arrival, that it would come out tonight. Plans were made. We can get you off the island. But, please, you have to promise never to come back." Holly's whispered voice kept him focused.

Kai moved quickly, keeping pace with his friend. "Who is 'we'?"

Holly looked back at him as she halted in front of a small door. "There's a small rowboat just down the path. We put your bow, some food, and a pouch of gold inside. Head to the docks, find Captain Ellory. He's expecting you as passenger. You'll sail as soon as you're on board."

Alaric's Bow: A Book of the Amari

Kai stopped her from darting off. "Who is this 'we' you keep talking of? Please, I need to know."

Her golden eyes no longer held back the tears. "Olive. She's our mother. Your true mother."

He knew what was going to happen to them once it came out they helped him escape. "Holly, come with me. I know what Kaerdan's going to do to the two of you."

"I can't." She lifted the hem of her skirt, displaying the iron band circling her ankle. Embracing him, she whispered, "Go, my brother. One of our family needs to remain unchained."

He put his hand to the lever, ready to raise it. "Holly, what's my name? I don't know any more."

She whispered in his ear, and then pushed him out the door.

Kai ran down the path, his ears straining to hear any pursuers. As promised, the small skiff waited for him. He pushed off, rowing with strong strokes. Escape mattered more than anything right now.

The docks were a short distance away, and he was running short on time. By now, the castle had been searched and

Alaric's Bow: A Book of the Amari

Kaerdan would be sending out parties to find him.

A lone figure stood on the closest pier, a massive merchant ship bobbing gently in the waves behind him. Three men appeared near the sandy beach, grabbing the bow and pulling him ashore. Kai grabbed at his bow and pack as he climbed out. The man he first saw approached.

"You the passenger I was told to expect?"

"Depends. Are you Captain Ellory?" The two men fell into step together, quickly moving across the dock and onto the ship.

"Aye, that I am. I understand there's a bit of a hurry to things. But can an old Captain know the name of his passenger?"

"The name's Alaric."

Alaric's Bow: A Book of the Amari

Chapter Three

The crossing would take over a week, which suited Alaric fine. He needed time to himself to decide what to do next.

Changing his name had been easy. Too easy. Ever since Holly whispered it in his ear, it felt right. More like who he was than Kai had ever been.

That first night, he'd mourned. Said good-bye to a mother and sister he'd never really known, who were most likely dead by now. If not dead, then they prayed for it swiftly. Kaerdan would punish them first. It was his way.

As to his other family, he scarcely thought on them. The feeling he'd had his entire life of being on the outside looking in made sense now. He didn't wholly belong there.

Nor was he fully Amari.

The second day was harder. Alaric stared at the polished brass mirror in his cabin for an hour, trying to see if there was any of the telltale gold coloring in his eyes. He'd heard of this, yes. Half-bred Amari were common enough, but almost all had the

Alaric's Bow: A Book of the Amari

eye color. He would be one of the very few who could pass as human.

While that would make things easier, he also knew what he couldn't do. Going to his grandfather's palace was out of the question. Even if a messenger didn't make it before he did, it wouldn't be far behind. No, Kai had to die. Disappear. Never to be seen or heard from again.

The crew left him alone, which suited him just fine. How Holly procured his passage he'd never know. He needed the time and solitude right now.

A light knock at the door to his small cabin roused him from his thoughts. He turned his head around as the door swung open, the wood creaking slightly. Captain Ellory slipped into the room, closing the door behind him.

"Pardon the intrusion, but something's happened you need to know about."

Alaric nodded, gesturing for the Captain to sit in the only chair in the room. He settled on his bunk, waiting.

Ellory sank into the chair. Alaric noticed both relief and concern on the man's weather-beaten face. Whether or not the man's gray hair was from age or worry he

Alaric's Bow: A Book of the Amari

couldn't tell. Outside of being older, there was no way to determine the Captain's age. Though, at eighteen, there many people who fit that statement.

"I know who you are, what you are. Holly and I go way back. I was the one who brought your mother, your real mother, to the Island. I've regretted every single trip your father took that ended with a chained Amari in the hold. Helping you escape isn't much, but it makes me feel better. The trick will be putting you ashore without anyone being the wiser."

Alaric nodded. "I know where not to go, but that's about it. I've never had to reinvent my life before." He ran a hand through his brown hair. "I'm fair with a bow. Maybe I could make my way to another King's holding, hide there as a hunter for his table."

Ellory shook his head. "Bad idea. Your brother won't stop until he's found you, made an example. You're a direct challenge to his rule. He'd like nothing more than to see you kneeling at his feet, a chain around your neck."

Shrugging, he replied, "He can have the entire island for all I care. I won't be going back there any time soon."

Alaric's Bow: A Book of the Amari

"Won't matter. Not to the likes of him. For all his bluster, he's an insecure brat. He knows you're a better man than he'll ever be. Until he can break you, he won't stop."

Pausing, the older man picked at a callous on the palm of his hand. "I've got another passenger. About your height, coloring. He died in the night." He held a hand up to stop Alaric's shocked words before they were spoken. "No, we didn't do anything to him. He was sick before he came on board. When we get to Lorien, we're going to swear that the passenger that died was a man we were hired to pick up in the dead of night. Near Caer Mikkel. The news will be reported to your Grandfather, who will send the message to your father and brother. And you can live your life."

Stunned, he absorbed the news. The Captain was handing him the chance to live without looking over his shoulder. "I don't know what to say…" he looked at the other man.

Ellory rose, holding out his hand in parting. Alaric grasped it in return. The captain slapped his shoulder with his free hand. "Go. Use that bow of yours, yes, but don't stay in one place too long. Rent it out

Alaric's Bow: A Book of the Amari

for private wars, mercenary work. You're alive, and we've made the best we can to cover your trail. Now you have to keep low enough to stay alive."

As the captain turned to leave, Alaric voiced the question he'd had on his mind for days. "Captain, why help me like this? What did Holly give you?"

A tired smile crossed the man's face. "Like I said, I owed a debt. Those of us who can hide tend to help those who need it."

Alaric's eyes grew wide as the pale blue of the captain's eyes fell away, briefly replaced by the telltale gold. Without another word, he watched the man walk out the door.

***

Two days later, he awoke to the sound of shouted orders and a flurry of footsteps on the deck above. Alaric pulled on his breeches as he stared out the small porthole. They'd arrived at Lorien.

He dressed quickly, choosing a green tunic. Holly had only packed three outfits, none of them anything that would proclaim his former rank. Maybe someday he'd be able to buy her freedom. But that would mean confronting Kaerdan.

Alaric's Bow: A Book of the Amari

"Put it from your mind, lad." Ellory's voice called out from the doorway. "You're not going to be able to save her. Her fate was sealed the moment she concocted your escape."

"You don't know that. Kaerdan might—" he started to say, shoving the last few belongings into his pack.

"No, he won't. You and I both know she's either dead, or wishing she was. And she knew it when she made her choice. Amari can't take any risks without repercussions, even those of us who are free. The magic we harness won't let us. There's always a price to be paid for our actions."

Alaric strapped his quiver to the side of his pack. "I can't accept that."

"Doesn't change it. If you want to repay her, then do what you can to save any Amari you run across. If you end up in an army, offer to watch over them. Show them kindness instead of brutality. And, if you ever find one who's stayed hidden and unchained, make sure they stay that way. Holly didn't give up her life so you could take her place in chains. She did it so her brother could save others."

Alaric looked away, slipping his pack onto his back. Ellory's words hit home.

Alaric's Bow: A Book of the Amari

He was right. Holly was either dead, or wished she were. Kaerdan wouldn't have been kind to her. Or Olive. The only one who might have been spared his wrath was his mother. His hand molded around the center of his bow through the covering. If nothing else in his life made sense, that still did.

"You may not have the eyes, Alaric. Be grateful for that. But you've got some sort of magic going on between you and that bow of yours. Just make sure the rest of the world thinks it's skill and nothing more. You might want to miss every now and then."

Pausing at the door, he held out his hand to the captain. "Thank you. For everything."

Ellory shook his hand. "You've got a debt to pay, lad. And you can't do that if you're in chains. Remember that."

Alaric nodded in understanding. Without another word, he wound his way up to the deck and then down to the dock.

He paid close attention to where he was going, dodging between stacks of crates, sailors, and laborers. The wooden platform below him swayed with movement

Alaric's Bow: A Book of the Amari

from above. The violent motion would've tripped him if it wasn't for the week at sea.

Stepping off the dock and onto the dirt road, he moved to one side. Partly to stay out of anyone's way, and so he could take a good look around him.

The city was laid out in a series of terraces cut into the hillside. The level people resided on depended on their rank. Situated at the top, looking down on everything, was his grandfather's palace. The white walls shimmered in the early morning sun. With a sigh, he realized it wasn't his grandfather that lived there. His welcome would be deceptively warm…right up until they chained him and put him on the first boat back to face Kaerdan.

He reached behind him and pulled the hood of his mantle over his head. There was no way of knowing if word had reached Lorien yet, but it wouldn't suit him to be reckless. He had to find a job, one that took him out of the city.

Alaric spent another few minutes studying the throng of people around him. Watching who moved where, who carried what.

"Pardon, sir, are you hungry?" a small voice piped up.

Alaric's Bow: A Book of the Amari

Looking down, he saw a young girl with a tray full of meat pies staring at him. Her gold eyes stood out on her dirty face. His stomach grumbled loudly. Laughing, he replied, "Well, there's your answer. How much for a pie?"

"They're a half crown, if you please. We just made them fresh this morning."

Reaching into his tunic, he pulled a coin out from a hidden pocket. Handing it to the child, he tried not to stare at the scars on her forearm. "There you are, one half crown. Do I get my pick?"

The girl quickly pocketed the money and held the tray a bit higher. "Yes, sir. Whichever one you'd like."

He barely had the pastry in his hand before she scampered off to another person. Poor child had been forced to use her magic already, and in ways that caused harm. Holly had taught him how it worked. How the magic rebounded on the Amari, scarring them in some way for the harm caused. His father had known about it, and never made them cause harm unless it was in self-defense. Whoever this child belonged to had no such morals.

He began to meander down the street, munching on the pastry as he walked.

Alaric's Bow: A Book of the Amari

If he could find a central market of some kind, join up with a caravan as a guard that would take him out of town.

After a few minutes, he knew enough of the area to realize he had to move inward. Closer to the city gates leading inland. The only people hiring near the docks wanted sailors. While he hadn't been sick on the crossing, he knew he wasn't cut out for that kind of life.

Two streets over, he heard the auctioneer's voice carry over the crowd around him. One last lot for the day. An Amari family. His chest tightened as he forced himself towards the market. A caravan heading inland would be perfect for him to hide in. And, if his luck held, he'd be able to help a few people along the way.

The crowd thinned out as he approached the small courtyard where the auction was being held. A few still stood in front of the wooden platform, absently raising a hand in answer to the auctioneer's bidding. A few others milled about a table, exchanging coin and signing parchment. Over to the left, against a stone building, a third man read over the parchments handed him and completed the transfer of

Alaric's Bow: A Book of the Amari

ownership. The whole thing, while done quietly and openly, turned Alaric's stomach.

The auctioneer called out, "Sold!" a final time, signaling the end of the day. Alaric watched the family of three being led off the platform. Another man stood not far from the bookkeeper's table. Alaric watched as he moved forward to pay. He was strong, sure. His beard hid most of his face. The robes he wore were long, nothing like anything Alaric had seen before. Vibrant colors in strange patterns. Wherever he was from, it wasn't close.

He continued to watch the robed man, waited until he finished the transfer and began to lead the family away from the market.

"Pardon, sir," Alaric stepped in front of the group. "I'm looking for work."

The man's brow furrowed slightly. "What kind of work?"

Shrugging, he responded. "About any I can find. Got a bit of a nagging need to see another part of the world."

"You any good with that thing?" The man pointed at the bow sticking up from the pack.

Alaric glanced back, noticed the covering had slipped loose. Looking forward

Alaric's Bow: A Book of the Amari

again, he said, "Good enough to help feed you and your men on the way home."

"We'll see. Earn your keep and you'll be paid when we arrive. Don't, and I'll leave you at the first hovel I care to."

"Fair enough. Where are we headed?

"Antioch. Hope you got good shoes, boy. You'll be walking in them for the next four months."

Alaric's Bow: A Book of the Amari

Chapter Four

Alaric woke, the morning sun blazing through the small window of his room. Three years in Antioch and he still wasn't used to the heat.

Rising, he poured some water from the ewer into the basin. Splashing the cool water over his face, he drew a deep breath. Every year, this day had been the hardest. The official visit from the Lorien contingent. He didn't go out of his way to draw notice to himself, never had. His skin had slowly darkened over the years, his brown hair lighter from the sun. The beard he now wore still itched, but he'd gotten used to it. Mostly.

Still, he kept his guard up. There was always the chance Kaerdan hadn't bought the lie that he died on the ship. His brother was nothing if not thorough. Until he saw a body, there was a chance Kai still lived.

Only no one here would know that name. To this city, he was Alaric. Still an Islander, yes. There was no way to hide that. But they'd accepted him, his story. At least, he hoped they had.

Alaric's Bow: A Book of the Amari

Knowing his absence along the procession route would be missed, he sighed. Erien wouldn't let him sit this one out. She'd asked so many questions when first they met about his home. In the beginning, he feared she was one of Kaerdan's spies. When the questions stopped and no one came, he relaxed a little. Erien had lived a life in this desert oasis is all. She dreamed of a land where water was plentiful. Though she scoffed at the idea of snow.

A light rapping at his door startled him. "Alaric, you up yet?" A female voice muffled by the thick wood.

"Yeah, hold on." He grabbed a caftan off of the peg on the wall. Tossing it over his head, he straightened out the folds as he walked toward the door.

Opening it, he was treated to a grin from his friend. "If I'd known you weren't dressed yet, I wouldn't have waited out here." Erien teased him.

"If I'd let you in while I was naked, your father would've had me drawn and quartered before the procession even started," he laughed in return. Closing the door behind him, he waited for her to move forward.

Alaric's Bow: A Book of the Amari

Her black hair, the long braid dangling down below her headscarf, swayed as she spoke. "Not if he knows what's good for him. The only hope he has for me to agree to any match he proposes for me is to not interfere with my friendships."

Alaric fell into step next to her, "Friendships? Is that the term they use around here?"

Erien laughed, "Not all the time, no. But Father and I worked out what I can and cannot do some time ago. He allows me the freedom to befriend those I want to, knowing nothing will become serious. And I accept a suitable candidate for my hand."

"The key word there being 'suitable', I suppose."

"Absolutely." She glanced back at him as they made their way down the narrow spiral staircase. "There's lots of men who would marry me simply because of who he is. I want someone who is more interested in who I am than his balance sheet."

"And some Islander doesn't count?"

She turned, craning her neck to meet his eyes. "Alaric, you know you have his trust and admiration. You earned that by finding food when no one else could on that

Alaric's Bow: A Book of the Amari

first caravan trip. But his position would be in jeopardy if he let us be together in that way. You and I both know his true nature. The rest of Antioch thinks of him as a ruthless slave trader. Even the Amari he brings back learn how to speak of him without lying but not telling of his kindness toward them. As long as Ajanor rules, and is friendly with Lorien, he cannot let his true nature show."

Alaric nodded. Ajanor was brutal when it came to how he treated the Amari. More died under his command each year. The treaty with Lorien was ironclad and suited both kingdoms well. The smaller kingdoms feared them, and rightly so. The wars waged had slowly chipped away at borders. In just the last three years, Antioch had annexed two of its neighbors. One didn't even bother to fight.

Lorien wasn't far behind. Rumor ran before the official visit, like always. Kaerdan now ruled the island with an iron fist. An alliance between him and Lorien seemed imminent, allowing Lorien access to the fleet of ships at his brother's command. Adding Antioch's forces to the mix would make it possible for war to ravage almost every kingdom in the world. What scared

Alaric's Bow: A Book of the Amari

him even more, though, was what would happen the day the alliance fell apart.

The bright sunlight exploded on them as Erien opened the door to the street outside. Alaric raised the hood of his caftan before stepping through the portal.

The avenue was already crowded with people eagerly awaiting the annual spectacle. The visit, long ago established as a reason to celebrate, drew hundreds from the neighboring towns as well as caravans from farther away. The massive desert had several oasis points, waystations for caravans that grew into thriving cities and towns. Coming to the capital, though, was reserved for only tradesmen. Except for when Lorien visited.

Had his room faced the street, Alaric would've been content to watch from above. Erien, however, loved being in the middle of it all. She fed off the energy of the crowd, enjoyed the spectacle. To her, the outfits worn by the visiting dignitaries were exotic. He could sympathize. It took him time to get used to wearing a caftan over breeches and a tunic.

They found a place and waited. It wasn't long before the trumpets blared, heralding the dignitaries. The parade wove

Alaric's Bow: A Book of the Amari

slowly past the throngs lining the streets. Musicians led the way, followed by a group of spearmen in full armor. The glare of the sun off the metal almost blinding those who looked too long. Then came the ornate, gilded litters. Each one sat on the shoulders of eight Amari men, clad in shirt and breeches. Alaric could see beads of sweat trickle down their faces as the heavy garments compounded the heat.

The curtains of each were pulled back, allowing the throngs to see the visitors in all their glory. Courtiers and diplomats lounged, richly embroidered and bejeweled fabrics clashed with the simplicity of the garments of those in the crowd. The fourth litter caused Alaric to clench his jaw.

Holly was one of the bearers, her head shaved. The tunic she wore, cut so no one would mistake her for a man, showed red skin with crisscrossed pale scars. The sun had been merciless to her during the journey, and so had Kaerdan.

She kept her eyes down as she passed. There was his brother, relaxing on a bed of satin pillows and a chalice in his hand. Nothing had changed in his appearance. The same arrogance and hard

Alaric's Bow: A Book of the Amari

set to the jaw remained. He refused to look outside at the people around him.

He felt Erien shift next to him, breaking his evaluation of Kaerdan. Her form retreated toward a doorway where her father stood, motioning to her.

Alaric slid between the crowd, trying to follow. By the time he reached her, she was alone. Her face held a look he'd never seen before. It wasn't quite fear or anger, but a bit of both.

She looked up and saw him. Holding a single hand up, she silenced him before he could say a word. "Not here, my friend. And not now. Go to work. I'll tell you before noon."

With that, he watched as she slipped away into the crowd.

He didn't see her again for two hours. He was in the back of the shop, working on some fletchings under the awning, when she sat next to him. Grabbing a small knife and a feather, she began to cut into the shaft.

They sat there in silence for a few moments. "I'm to be married. Soon. My husband," contempt dripped from her voice, "is among the diplomats and is eager to take me home with him."

Alaric's Bow: A Book of the Amari

Alaric's gut tightened. "I thought you were granted the right to refuse a suitor."

"I was, initially. But now Ajanor has stepped in. He wants this alliance, and Father dared not refuse him."

He swallowed, fearing her answer to his next question. "Who is it to be, then? Some minor bureaucrat?"

She sighed. "No. Someone who claims to be King of the Islanders. Seems his wife died giving birth to a daughter two years ago and he's done grieving. That same daughter is now betrothed to one of Ajanor's younger sons. I'm part of the deal to secure the treaty." Angrily, she swiped the blade across the shaft of the feather. "Bartered and sold like an Amari, only with marriage vows binding me over a steel band around my ankle."

Alaric didn't dare speak. It could only be Kaerdan. Fear for his friend overtook him. "So, run. Leave. If you don't want this Island King, don't wed him."

The knife flew from her hand, lodging in a barrel across from them. "I can't. You and I both know this. I'm bound to obey my father and my King. This is the price I pay for the life I live."

Alaric's Bow: A Book of the Amari

Unable to contain himself, Alaric turned to her. He grabbed one of her hands and held it close. "Erien, don't do this. You don't know him. You'll regret this faster than you can imagine."

She snorted, "Strange words from an Islander. I always thought you saw your kings as gods walking the land." She pulled her hand from his. "It doesn't matter. The announcement is being made tonight, at the feast. Father asks that you attend, as well. He thinks showing this King he has Islanders under his employ will increase his position."

Alaric's eyes widened briefly. "He wants me there? No. I can't." He rose, a hand flying to his brow. His head was pounding faster than his heart.

"Alaric, what's wrong? You've never denied an invitation like this before. It's obvious you know my husband-to-be. If there's something my father should know, that I should know, about him then say it."

"I can't, Erien. You and your father know enough. I left the Island, and my life there, with reason. If Kaerdan were to even suspect I was here—"

"Erien, leave us." Rahjin's voice called out from the doorway. "This is a

Alaric's Bow: A Book of the Amari

matter for men. Your mother waits on you to start preparations for the feast."

Alaric didn't turn as Erien left to obey her father's command. He didn't dare.

"If there is a tale I must hear, tell it now, Islander. Otherwise, your presence is needed tonight as I celebrate the coming marriage. I have let you live among my family for long enough now that you should trust me. Give me reason to excuse you from the feast that I can abide by."

Defeated, Alaric slumped onto a bench. "What do you know, Rahjin? Or guessed?"

The older man sat opposite him. "I know the story you gave on the way here was full of half-truths. That you are an Islander there is no doubt. From the north? I do not think so. The cloak you had wasn't thick enough to hold back the cold they face. Your skill with a bow was almost too good. While many from your lands can hunt well, you rarely missed. Even when the other hunters came back claiming there was no beast to be found, you'd find something. My next trip, you refused to go back to Lorien. I asked around. Seems the same time you showed up the year earlier, there were rumors about the new King having a half-

Alaric's Bow: A Book of the Amari

Amari brother. One they thought was dead. But no corpse was found."

Alaric nodded, "You're not a foolish man, Rahjin. Kaerdan would repay you handsomely for turning me over. He may even agree not to beat your daughter once they're married."

"You are family, Alaric. You reside in my home, work for me. I will hold your secret. And excuse you from the feasting. Though I recommend you find a way out of the city soon. You, and your bow, will be missed. But your brother will find out about you if you remain. Too many others will remark about an Islander in my employ if you stay. As to Erien," he paused, "make no mistake. If I hear he has mistreated her in any way, the next breath he draws will be his last. And she will rule the Island then, not him." Rahjin rose. "Go. Pack your gear and find a tavern. Hire yourself off as a personal guard to someone else leaving the city. More are leaving than coming in now. I wish you well, my friend." He held out his hand to Alaric.

Grasping it, Alaric nodded. "Thank you. Tell Erien, well, tell her to ask for a gift from Kaerdan. There's an Amari with his

Alaric's Bow: A Book of the Amari

party, a woman by the name of Holly. She'll serve Erien well."

"Any message you want sent to her?"

He shook his head. "No. It'll only put both of them at risk. Better she thinks her brother is dead, and Erien not know at all, than otherwise." He paused. "Thank you, again. You've given me refuge when it was needed. I won't forget that."

"Repay my kindness by doing the same for another. You'd do well as a mercenary, Alaric. As long as the cause is a just one."

Alaric walked into the shop without another word. Rahjin was right. He had to disappear. No good-byes. For the second time in less than four years, he was running. Only this time, he had allies to cover his trail.

Darting up the stairs to his small room, his mind raced. What to pack, what to leave behind. It really wasn't a hard decision. He knew he had to leave, tonight if possible. The months on the road to reach Antioch taught him what was important to carry with him. He'd not collected much since he lived here, either.

Alaric's Bow: A Book of the Amari

The packing was swift. He made sure his tunic and breeches were closer to the top this time, along with a razor. He changed into his sturdy leather boots, then moved aside the small chest of drawers. In the wall behind it, he worked the tip of his dagger into a barely noticeable gap in the boards. Reaching into the space, he pulled out two pouches full of coin. The benefit of never buying more than one needed. He had money for the journey ahead.

He secured one pouch deep within the pack, under several layers of clothing. His repair kit slid into a pocket next to the strap meant for his quiver. Carefully, he secured the wrapping around his bow. He wasn't sure if Kaerdan would recognize the carving, but now was not a time to take chances.

One last look around the room that had been home for three years to make sure everything necessary was packed. Shouldering his burden, he walked out the door without looking back.

Alaric's Bow: A Book of the Amari

Chapter Five

The tavern was full, even in this part of Antioch. Revelers mixed with thieves and pickpockets, each offering toasts to the happy couple. And the alliance in general. War was coming, and with it the chance for more profit.

Alaric kept to himself in a corner. He'd been here for two days now. No one was hiring, not yet. Wait a few days, they said. We want to celebrate first. The longer he waited, the more nervous he became.

One way or another, he was leaving by dawn. Even if it meant buying a camel. The next big city was still a good three days to the south. A horse was faster, but that meant extra feed, water. The camel could do the distance.

The wedding procession had wound through the streets that evening. Alaric stayed in his corner, avoiding the spectacle. Ale was his friend tonight. Though the three pints he'd downed so far had done little to dull the pain he felt.

Alaric's Bow: A Book of the Amari

He wasn't so far gone he couldn't keep an eye on his things, though. Or not pick up on small changes in the tavern. He saw the urchin who stole coin out of one pocket while pretending to wipe up crumbs, and the barkeep adding water to the keg when he thought no one was looking. Most of the guests, though, were too busy celebrating.

Not all, though. A group of four sat at a table in the opposite corner. Two women, two men. Warriors, a probable thief, and someone he couldn't figure out. Important, though, the way the other three watched around her. The red braid hanging straight down her back stood out like a beacon. More than one man approached the table, hoping to find out who she was. Each time, they were rebuffed by the other three.

"Entire town reeks right now, I'm telling you. Wish that Islander would take his Amari and leave already. It's bad enough with the ones that live here. This stinkin' lot can't even teach them to bathe." Alaric heard the bitter words of the man the next table over. He sipped at his ale, listening.

"What'cha talkin' about, Charlie? The foreigners are cleaner than you've ever been." Laughter overtook the group.

Alaric's Bow: A Book of the Amari

"Those Amari, they've got a smell about them. Not everyone can tell, but I can. It has to do with the magic they do. Especially the ones that are unchained. People need to leash their pets, you know. Otherwise they might get 'lost'."

More laughter erupted from the group. "Doubt there's any free for the takin' in this place, Charlie. Ajanor's stricter than most on his pets. Don't you remember? When we crossed into his lands last year, the checkpoints we had to go through. The man's paranoid that some unchained Amari's going to murder him in his sleep."

Out of the corner of his eye, Alaric watched the man they called Charlie shrug. "No skin off my nose if he's paranoid. I'm just tired of the stench. Can even smell it in here, and there's not a single one to be seen."

Trumpets blared outside. Alaric stayed seated while most of the room filed outside to see why. He knew why. The ceremony was finally over. Erien and her new husband were being paraded through the streets. He knew himself well enough to stay seated. Otherwise, he might do something he knew he'd regret.

Alaric's Bow: A Book of the Amari

He absently stared at the inside of his mug, watching the ale swirl around the bottom. He hated living in the shadows, watching life happen around him. All because others thought he was worth saving. Right now, he felt like he was the last person who should be saved. But he had no way of saving anyone else.

Another person slid into the seat opposite of him. "I hear you're looking for a job."

Raising his head, Alaric studied the older man. He'd been with the others, across the room. His dark hair blended with the collar of the tunic he wore. It was the thief.

"I might be. What's the job?"

"Just get myself and my companions to the border of Dunegan. Only a week or two at most, depending on how fast we travel. We're not familiar with travel in the desert and need a guide." The man's dark gaze was piercing. Whoever he was, he would know when Alaric was lying.

"When do we leave?"

The other man placed a hand on the table, pushing himself up. "Now. We're not big on celebrations, and we'd like to be on our way."

Alaric's Bow: A Book of the Amari

Alaric stood as well, though swaying slightly. "Fair enough." Grabbing his pack and wrapped bow, he followed the other man through the doorway.

The rest of the group were mounted on three horses. A fourth animal was saddled and waiting. A pack mule, laden with supplies, was led by the other man. The man who hired him vaulted up behind the red-haired woman. Her covering hid most of her features, and she kept her head down. Alaric moved toward the waiting horse. "You hired the drunk?" The other woman snorted.

"Something tells me he's going to be fine when he's sober, Gwen. And that he needs to leave here more than we do. You can ask him questions over dinner if you want. But the decision's mine." The man looked over at Alaric. "I'm Emile. That's Gwen." He nodded to the woman on the other horse. "Trystian's going to bring up the back with the supplies. We'll follow you." Emile nodded, expecting Alaric to take point.

He maneuvered his horse closer to Emile's. "What's your name, miss?" he asked the woman riding in front.

Alaric's Bow: A Book of the Amari

Her head swiveled. A pair of green eyes set in a pale face met his gaze. There was no fear, only a tired resignation in them. "It's Fin," she replied softly.

"Questions can wait. You were hired to lead us to the border. Let's go." Emile's voice was direct, commanding.

Alaric nodded. Whoever this Fin was, the rest were determined to protect her. He got the sinking feeling he'd just signed on for something far more dangerous than he originally thought.

***

Alaric held up his hand, signaling the group to stop. "We rest here. It's going to be too dark to keep going within an hour. And too cold." He turned in his saddle. "There's no oasis we can reach for at least a day's ride. The rocks over there—" he pointed to his left "—we put the tent against them. They'll shield us from any storms in the night." He guided his horse toward the formation, hearing the others follow behind.

Four hours of silence had marked the journey so far. He was sober now, not that it mattered. He wasn't that far into his cups to begin with. He knew the way to Dunegan, and how to get there safely. This part of the

Alaric's Bow: A Book of the Amari

desert was tricky. Even the raiders stayed away most of the time.

Alaric busied himself with making a way for them to tether the horses for the night while the others erected the tent on the sheltered side of the rocks. "Is it safe for a fire?" Emile asked.

He nodded his head. "Should be, if you keep it small. Raiders, if they come, will wait for us to be farther from the city."

"We still keep watch." Trystian's deep voice was barely over a whisper.

"I don't think that's what he was suggesting, Trystian." Alaric raised his head at the sound of the woman's voice. Calm, soothing. And tired. Whoever this Fin was, she wasn't immune to that.

Emile led the woman over to a chair, making her sit. Gwen handed her a water skin. A whispered command of "Rest now, we've got things covered" as she did so.

Alaric tore his gaze from her. "I recommend we keep the horses saddled, though. Just in case." He kept his focus on the animals, but watched as the others put the tent up quickly. One side was left open, the canvas stretched out to give some shelter to the horses.

Alaric's Bow: A Book of the Amari

The large, bearded man called Trystian had a fire started by the time Alaric finished tending to the horses. A small pot, suspended over the flames, showed promise of a good meal. It wouldn't be much, but it'd be hot and filling.

Alaric set up his bedroll for the night. Not so close to the others that there'd be cause for alarm, but still within the shelter of the tent. He already knew they didn't trust him yet. No reason to push it.

"How long do you think we'll be on the road, Islander?" Gwen didn't look at him as she spoke.

He shrugged. "Depends. If we don't encounter any trouble, no more than a week. If we get caught up in a storm, could be two."

"Do raiders come through often?"

"They're usually more active closer to whatever oasis they operate from. If we stay on the main road, take no shortcuts, they probably won't bother us. I don't care much for Ajanor's policies, but he did right by having the army patrol the main route. If we put a coin or two into the right hands as we move along, no one will bother us."

Alaric's Bow: A Book of the Amari

Emile spoke up. "No worries there. I've got coin for that. I'd rather bribe a few officials than be set on in the night."

"Raiders are the least of our worries at night," Trystian's deep voice carried in the still night air. Glancing at the man, Alaric saw him raise his dagger. A large scorpion writhed on the tip. The black and red striped body made him swallow hard.

"Those are the worst out here. Can kill a man with a single jab, but rarely come near humans. If we keep the fire going, they'll stay away." Alaric stated with conviction.

"Hope so. If they get to one of the horses, you're the one walking the next day." Trystian pointed with his dagger, emphasizing his words. "Food's ready." He flicked the blade in his hand, sending the dead scorpion off into the night.

Conversation was sparse over the meal. Emile set up a rotation, but didn't mention Alaric in it. Not surprising, really. He was the guide, that's it. That he needed to get out of Antioch as badly as they seemed to want to wasn't mentioned.

He settled into his bedroll, staring at the sky for a time. Thousands of stars shone down on him. His mind drifted to Erien. It was her wedding night. Was Kaerdan being gentle with her? By the gods, he hoped so.

"You trust him." Fin's whispered voice reached his ears.

"Yes." Emile replied. "So will you, in time. It won't be any different than when Gwen or Trystian came across our path."

"I'm not so sure. There's something different about him." Alaric heard the hesitation in her voice.

"You still trust me, don't you?"

"Of course. Just as I have since you found me."

"Well, then. You trust me. I trust him. He's got almost as much to fear as you do, Fin. He's no slaver."

She muttered something else he couldn't understand. Whatever it was, the conversation was over.

Shrugging it off, he closed his eyes. They provided him a way out of Antioch. Away from any chance of Kaerdan finding him. Whatever secrets they had would either come out in the journey ahead, or not at all. One final prayer in hopes that Erien's life would not be what he feared it would be, and he let sleep overtake his body.

"Wake up, slowly. We have company." The whispered command drove

Alaric's Bow: A Book of the Amari

sleep from his mind. Blinking, he stared up at the stars. Still an hour or two before sunrise. The horses pranced nervously. A dark figure, his back against the rocks near him, nodded once. "They're coming, slowly, from the road. Don't know they've been seen. Only five of them. Trystian, Gwen, and I will deal with them. Stay here, watch over Fin." Emile turned to him, his face a deadly mask. "If any of them get through us, put her on a horse and go. We'll catch up. If she's taken while there's still breath in your body, Islander, you'll wish you'd never heard of us."

Alaric eased out of his blankets, reaching for his bow as he rose. He kept his back to the road as he unwrapped it from the casing and slid the string into place. He took a moment to watch as Emile slid into the tent to wake the others. The two warriors rose with a practiced stealthiness, strapping on a few bits of armor too cumbersome to sleep in. Emile blocked his view of Fin.

Trying to move naturally, he sauntered the few feet to the horses. He'd left his quiver strapped to the saddle. Given the tenor of Emile's instructions, he pulled out just a few arrows. If they had to run for it, he'd need most to discourage pursuit.

Alaric's Bow: A Book of the Amari

Without warning, Trystian came charging out of the darkness of the tent, screaming. Gwen followed, bellowing a war cry that would scare the very rocks. Alaric barely spotted Emile slipping around the edges of the outcropping.

Alaric moved toward the opening of the tent. He stabbed five arrows into the ground so he could easily grab them, and notched a sixth. Their attackers were in range, but the shadows were still too deep to recognize friend from foe.

He heard Fin moving up behind him. "Stay back. I don't want to shoot you by accident."

Her exhale was more of a hiss than anything. "I can defend myself, even if he doesn't think so!"

Alaric thrust out his arm, blocking her stride. "Doesn't matter. And I never said you couldn't. But I'd rather piss you off than Emile. Something tells me he's deadlier than you."

He took his eyes off the combat to look at her. The red hair glowed in the faint light, framing her narrow face. Her green eyes glared at him, ready for a fight. He swallowed. Perhaps she was the deadlier of the two.

Alaric's Bow: A Book of the Amari

He nodded once as she stepped back, eyes still blazing with anger. The light was enough now to determine the combatants. He raised the bow, slowly drawing the string back to his ear. Taking aim, he released the arrow at precisely the right time, piercing one of the raiders through the neck as he moved in behind Gwen.

Snatching an arrow from the ground in front of him, he drew back again and let it fly. This one caught the raider mid-thigh, distracting him enough for Trystian's sword to get through his defenses.

A heavy thud reverberated through the ground behind him, followed by Fin's startled gasp. He grabbed another arrow as he pivoted, letting it fly as soon as he saw the back of the raider. The man screamed, letting loose his hold on Fin. A sword slashed toward Alaric's midsection, barely missing his tunic. He dropped the bow and drew out a dagger. "Fin! Get on my horse. Now!" he ordered, dodging another attack.

He kicked the bow toward her. His attention went off his opponent for a moment as he watched her grab it as she ran past. A searing pain bit into his left shoulder as the sword found a mark. Without thought, he drove forward and plunged his dagger

Alaric's Bow: A Book of the Amari

into the raider's chest. His foe dropped to the ground, dead. Alaric grabbed the remaining arrows and headed to the horses. His vision blurred. The world spun, and then darkness overtook him.

Alaric's Bow: A Book of the Amari

Chapter Six

He didn't remember much. A fever, perhaps? Nightmares that made him sweat? He only knew pain that wouldn't end. And a voice that talked him through the black abyss.

The first few times he heard it, he couldn't place it. It was a woman's voice. Holly? Erien? Whoever it was, they told him to fight. Not to give in.

The darkness was so comfortable, though. It surrounded him like a blanket, cocooning him in warmth and security. He didn't have any worries here. No pain, no fears. Kaerdan wouldn't find him, ever. And it tempted him with that promise.

But still that soft voice persuaded him, coaxed him to shed the bindings around him. It was that voice that peeled away the layers of darkness.

As they left, the pain returned. Searing through his muscles, making him scream. It burned throughout his blood, tearing through his organs with jagged teeth. The woman's voice remained steady as his back arched and the sweat streamed down

Alaric's Bow: A Book of the Amari

his face. Hours went by before sleep offered him an escape from the delirium.

How long he slept, he didn't know. Emile's voice was the first one to pierce the recesses of his brain, though.

"You're sure he's going to be able to travel soon? We can't stay here much longer, Fin. Gwen and Trystian aren't going to be able to keep everything away."

A woman answered, the same voice that had coaxed him back from death. "I'm sure. His wound's healed. If he was going to succumb to the venom, he would've done so by now." Fin replied. Weariness tinged her words.

"And what about you?" Emile's voice was softer now, concerned. "Are you recovered enough to travel safely?"

"I'll be fine, Emile. I trust you won't let me slide off the horse if I fall asleep while we ride." She chuckled. There was something in the laugh that gave Alaric strength. She didn't laugh nearly as much as she should, he realized. An idea began to form in his head, pieces of a puzzle falling into place.

"And Alaric? Do you trust him now?"

Alaric's Bow: A Book of the Amari

He heard someone shift. "Yes. I don't know what he remembers, but I saw enough to trust him. Few would do what he did. Even fewer would live through it."

Her words reverberated through his skull, unlocking that which the pain had blocked out. How he'd killed the fighter and ran toward her, intent on getting her to safety like Emile made him swear to do. Seeing the scorpion crawling up the back of the horse. And not caring how many times it jabbed him as he pulled it off and crushed it. The horror on her face as he blacked out. The last thing he saw was her kneeling at his side, the green eyes shifting into gold.

She was Amari.

"Planning on eavesdropping some more, Islander? Or are you ready to admit you're awake?" Emile wasn't quite joking.

Carefully, Alaric sat up. The right arm of his tunic was ripped away at the shoulder, a line of stitches decorated his skin.

"We had Gwen do that. Visual clues of healing are better received by wandering groups over…"

"Over knowing we have an Amari with us? One that's unchained?" Alaric finished Emile's sentence for him.

Alaric's Bow: A Book of the Amari

Fin snorted, "See, Emile? I told you he wasn't stupid."

Emile stared at him, and chose his words carefully. "Now you know. And I know about you, Islander. I don't hire anyone without checking out their background. You need to stay on the move, remain hidden, as much as Fin does. Stay on with us, if you want. We'll protect your secrets as long as you protect her. The minute you betray that, I have no reason not to hand you over to your brother. Or what's left of you."

Alaric nodded, "And what if we mutually decide to part ways?" He knew, the moment he said the words he would never leave Fin's side. But he still had to ask.

Shrugging, Emile responded, "Then we still agree to keep each other's secrets. Fin's lived a life free, Alaric. Much like you have. She's never been anyone's pet, never felt the band of metal enslave her. Make sure it continues, even if our paths move apart, and I promise you'll never have to face your brother unless you choose to."

He looked over at Fin. "Are you agreeable to this?"

She raised her head to meet his gaze. The green coloring was back. "I've trusted

Alaric's Bow: A Book of the Amari

Emile for as long as I can remember. He's kept me safe, unchained, this long. If he trusts you, so do I." Turning, her red braid swinging with the movement, Fin started to shove a few things into a pack.

Alaric started to go help her, but a hand on his arm stopped him. Emile smiled, "That's not the way, Islander. She can care for herself in most ways. She's strong, tough. Has needed to be. Don't ever let her think you don't know that." He thrust a chin toward the pallet Alaric had been sleeping on. "Just pack up your bedding and get your gear together. I'll let the others know we're ready to head out."

"Hey, Emile, how long was I out?"

"Three days." Emile disappeared around the open end of the tent.

Alaric blinked, trying to reconnect his thoughts to the lost days. Nothing but pain filled his mind. Shaking his head to clear the thought, he gave up. It wasn't like he could go back and change what happened. Indeed, he probably wouldn't. Three days at the outcropping, though. Emile was right. They had to move onward. Even if they'd kept raiders at bay, there would've been curious travelers.

Alaric's Bow: A Book of the Amari

"Not many, really. One or two, yes. But Gwen would talk to them, get them to move along. No one outside of that first group that gave us any trouble." Fin said.

"Reading my mind?" He joked. And instantly regretted it as her jaw set in a rigid line.

"No, Islander. I don't read minds. I'm not a seer." She didn't even bother to try and hide her irritation.

"Fin, I'm sorry. I didn't mean to imply anything."

She brushed past him, her tightly wrapped bedroll in her arms. "If you don't mean it, don't say it, Islander."

"My name's Alaric." He knotted up the rope, securing his bedding, and rose from the ground.

She was with the pack horse. "Not for a while it's not. Alaric has to disappear for a time. Give your brother time to forget any possible connections between you and Kai. Build up the reputation of an Islander that's good with a bow for now. In a year or so, the connection with your name will be a bowman, not a fugitive."

He nodded. "So, the names you all have. Those are aliases as well?"

Alaric's Bow: A Book of the Amari

She moved back and forth from the tent, bringing out packs and other items and placing them in a pile near the horses. "Bring everything out first, then we load while Trystian and Gwen take down the tent," she instructed.

They worked in silence for a few minutes. Alaric was still curious, but wasn't willing to push the issue. Finally, when everything was out, she began to instruct him on what to bring to her as she loaded up the animal. "Yes and no. Some of us shortened our names out of necessity. Others changed it because we're escaping a life we knew was wrong for us." She strapped a pack into place. "You'll learn what you need to know as we travel, I'm sure. We're all trying to escape something, Islander. In that, the five of us have a common goal."

"More than keeping you free, you mean." He didn't shy away from the statement. Fin's entire speech had been very factual, straightforward. She wasn't one to ignore reality.

She looked over the saddle at him, "Exactly. I don't know all of the stories. Emile does the research, found Gwen and Trystian much as he did you. He makes the

Alaric's Bow: A Book of the Amari

decisions. I just follow them. It's easier that way."

He waited until the last item was off the ground, then reached a hand out to touch hers. "If I caused you pain, I apologize. What you did for me…well, I'm grateful."

She slid her hand out from under his and avoided his gaze. "It wasn't bad. It was healing I performed, not harm. My head felt like it was about to split open for a few hours, but no scarring. That only happens when we hurt another."

"Trystian, don't stand under the tent when we're taking it down!" Gwen's exasperated voice called out, jarring Alaric for a moment. He'd forgotten they weren't alone.

No one spoke much while the rest of the camp was torn down. Alaric stayed out of the way, waiting and watching. Everyone knew what to do, trying to help would only result in him getting in the way. So, he kept his eyes open, and dagger out, for more scorpions. They rarely came out during the day, though. But he was wary all the same.

"Islander, what's the chance we meet up with more of the bugs you squashed when we stop tonight?" Trystian called out

Alaric's Bow: A Book of the Amari

as the last pole was secured to the pack horse.

Alaric swung up into his saddle. Grasping the reins, he replied, "Slim to none. There's either an oasis or outpost we can stop at each night the rest of the way to the border. We left too late earlier to make it safely or we wouldn't have needed to stop here."

Gwen settled her horse as it pranced, anxious to get moving after the days of inactivity. "What's the situation like at these places?"

Emile answered before Alaric could. "Nothing we haven't encountered before, Gwen. He already told us. Coins in the right hands and no one will know we've passed by."

She snorted, "Not until someone pays more, you mean." She pressed her heels into the animal's flanks and headed toward the road.

Alaric looked toward Emile, who waved him forward. He wanted to talk with Fin more, but it wasn't going to happen as long as she rode with Emile.

Alaric's Bow: A Book of the Amari

Alaric's Bow: A Book of the Amari

Chapter Seven

Dawn broke at some point, but it only changed the shade of grey in the clouds. The rainy season had hit Dunegan's western lands hard. Four months of steady rain, varied only by severity and wind. They'd spent three years in this country, moving every six months or so. Never spending too much time in one village to raise suspicion about Fin. Or any of them for that matter.

Alaric still wasn't thrilled with where Emile wanted them to go next. Lorien. But he hadn't steered them wrong yet. Held up his end of their bargain. It had taken a year to bury the rumor of the lost prince of the Islands. Another for "Islander" to become synonymous with his new name, and skill with a bow. This last year, they'd finally gotten settled in. Trystian had taken up with a young woman in Evenshire, their latest home. Things were encouraging. There were no Amari to be seen. And that meant no slavers waiting to turn Fin into a pet. Or chain Alaric and send him back to face his brother.

Outside of Fin and Emile, no one knew his parentage. He had no clue if

Alaric's Bow: A Book of the Amari

Trystian and Gwen knew. If they did, nothing was said. He didn't have the outward signs, did no magic.

Unless you counted his aim. He had grown deadly with his bow, using his marksmanship to both keep them fed and earn their keep as they moved around. The beard was gone, his brown hair longer. Six years on the run now, and his body had changed. He was no longer some soft prince, used to feather beds and savory meals. He was leaner now, more muscle than fat. Wary and suspicious of everyone they met. And, as always, watching out for Fin's safety.

He leaned against the window frame now, alert. Wishing the rain would let up enough they could get back on the road. The others slept on cots behind him. They'd left Evenshire a week ago, after Trystian's lady had begun asking questions. About Fin, Emile. Why he traveled with such companions, took on such danger to protect one person. Emile was fairly certain it was jealousy, but didn't want to wait to have that confirmed. Trystian could've stayed if he wanted to. Instead, he bid his lady good-bye. Told her he'd be back one day, when his task was complete. Alaric knew his

Alaric's Bow: A Book of the Amari

companion would keep that vow. He wasn't so certain about the lady.

They got as far as the inn, the last bit of Dunegan hospitality before crossing over to Lorien. The capital was a good month or more west. He prayed Emile would choose to go around the city. Somehow, he doubted it.

"Is it dawn yet?" Fin called out softly from behind him.

Turning, Alaric glanced at her. Her red hair half unbraided, she lay on her cot. Not ready to get up, really, but done sleeping.

"I think so. The clouds are lighter." He kept his voice low so he didn't wake the others.

She threw aside the blanket and sat up, stretching. Her tunic, wrinkled by sleep, hid her slender form. Alaric quickly looked back outside. Thoughts of what might be under that tunic still in his mind.

He heard her moving about, pulling on a pair of trousers. Their life didn't allow for fancy dresses she once told him. It was far more practical to ride in breeches. There was one night, a year ago. A celebration in a town square. She and Gwen had both agreed to dress in borrowed gowns for the event, as

Alaric's Bow: A Book of the Amari

they didn't want to anger the man who was letting them stay in the barn and work for a few coins. It was the first time, the only time, he'd seen her dressed up.

The sight of her in the blue dress burned in his mind. A woman's body rested under the corseted top, one that took his breath away.

She leaned against the wall across from him, her fingers deftly undoing the braid. "It's been doing this for days. We're not going to get to Lorien in time if we don't leave soon."

"In time?" he asked. "I didn't know we had a deadline."

Fin shrugged, "It's an anniversary of sorts. Emile and I go back there every ten years. He found me there. I don't know if he's hoping he'll find another to keep free or what, but he's insisted we go back." She finished undoing her hair and shook it loose. "Not that it's a huge thing. This is only the second trip."

"You and Emile have been together since you were three?"

She smiled. "You sound surprised. I think he was about 16 or so. Found me in the sewers. I'd convinced myself that hiding in all the muck would keep me safe."

Alaric's Bow: A Book of the Amari

There was an unspoken rule among the group. No one asked about their lives before they came together. It was as if the past didn't exist before they promised to keep Fin safe. In the quiet of the morning, though, it seemed right.

"Do you remember anything before then? About your parents? Where you lived?"

"No, not really." Her fingers began to braid her hair again. "Vague images of being in a small boat and being very afraid that someone would find me. All my energy went to changing my eyes green for the first few years. Hiding who I am, what I am. So much so that it's instinctive now."

"It's not right, you know. Amari shouldn't have to hide who they are. They should be free like everyone else."

"It's easier for you. I've run into other half Amari. Every one of them had the gold eyes, even if they didn't have the access to magic. You got your father's eyes instead." There was a bitterness to her voice.

"I still feel the same way, Fin. No one should ever be a pet, a slave, to another. The way some force the Amari to use their magic. It's barbaric."

"Like your brother?"

Alaric's Bow: A Book of the Amari

He stared out into the gloomy morning, his jaw clenched. Rumors had reached them over the last few years. Wars fought by Kaerdan and Ajanor, where the Amari dead rivaled the foot soldiers. More and more of the surrounding kingdoms were falling to their forces. And tensions within the alliance grew as well.

Then the news came that Kaerdan's grandfather, the ruler of Lorien, had died after a prolonged illness. His brother now had a major foothold on the mainland that was under his direct control. No more rallying troops under his grandfather's banner. It was his now. And that was a cold reality for Alaric.

"Kaerdan was never one to think of the Amari as anything but a means to an end. For him, that was power." He looked at Fin, "I'm not like him. Even when I didn't know about my real mother. And it's not what he learned from our father."

Her green eyes met his gaze. He still yearned for another glance of the gold. "If Emile ever thought you were, he would've slit your throat while you slept." The steel of her words spoke volumes. Even after these years, the trust wasn't there.

Alaric's Bow: A Book of the Amari

"Don't scare him, Fin." Emile's voice carried from his cot. "He's not stupid. He knows what he signed up for."

A small smile played across Fin's face, the quickest upturn of the lips that Alaric barely caught. Had she been teasing him?

"Emile, there's a shop in town with some archery supplies. I need to restock what I have. What do you think of picking up a bow for Fin?"

She started, interest and fear warring on her face. He turned his head toward the center of the room. "It's a bit too obvious for her to be with us and not have any fighting skills. Anyone would be able to pick her out as the one being protected if we're all combatants and she's not. We get her outfitted with a bow, some flint tipped arrows. I can give her lessons at night during the watch. She may not hit much, but she'll at least look the part."

Emile nodded. "Good idea. I should've thought of that myself." He held up a hand, "Don't argue, Fin. It's decided. The three of us will go right after breakfast. Trystian and Gwen can pack up. Rain or no rain, we head out today."

Alaric's Bow: A Book of the Amari

Alaric watched as Fin eased out of her position on the windowsill. He knew his interest in her was starting to go beyond any sort of promise he made Emile. He wanted to keep her safe now for his own reasons.

Not that she couldn't protect herself. The few times he'd seen her tap into her magic went beyond extraordinary. That he lived through the scorpion's sting still left him in awe. He shuddered to think what Kaerdan would do with her. He'd use her to level entire kingdoms, never caring about the scars or pain it caused her. If his brother ever made a pet of Fin, she'd be dead within a year. Probably less.

And Alaric knew he'd kneel in front of his brother in a heartbeat if it kept her free.

Rising, he casually made his way to his pack. Trystian and Gwen were waking up at Emile's urging. They'd go down as a group, eat. Then he'd lead Emile and Fin the short distance to the shop he'd been told about. He rummaged through his kit, making mental notes about what he needed for himself. Good quality catgut or bowstrings were hard to come by, and expensive, but worth the price. Buy cheap, regret it later

Alaric's Bow: A Book of the Amari

when the string breaks when your life depends on it.

"You really think I can shoot a bow?" Fin's voice drifted past his ear.

He turned his head and smiled at her. "Absolutely. It's not that hard. You could even learn how to miss on purpose if you wanted to."

She shrugged, the red hair moving in a way that made him want to reach out and stroke it. "I think I'll be plenty good at missing my target. But you and Emile are right. I need to learn, if for no other reason than to take the attention off of myself." She looked down at her hands. "Any chance I can get some gloves? I've seen the callouses on your hands. They won't happen overnight, and I won't heal myself."

"Why not?" he asked, puzzled. "If I could do what you can, it would make sense to me to do it."

Her mouth turned up slightly, a wistfulness crossing her face. "We can't, Alaric. Amari can do magic, yes. But only to others. Trying to heal myself would be as impossible as it would be for you to shoot yourself in the back. It just can't happen." A small twinkle danced in her green eyes. "And who says you can't do a kind of

Alaric's Bow: A Book of the Amari

magic? You may not look like your mother, but your aim is almost inhuman. Surely there's something beyond skill in that."

It was Alaric's turn to shrug. "Who can say, really?
Even if there's a bit more to it than skill, I don't have any of your disadvantages. I can kill without scars."

"You aren't doing the killing. The arrow is. There's a difference." Her tone echoed a despair he couldn't really fathom.

"Fin, you don't have to answer this. But...have you?"

"Have I ever killed someone? No. Not yet. I've come close, but Emile stepped in first. But I do have scars. Some hurt more than others when I got them."

He knew better than to pursue the topic. A sadness radiated from her now, making his heart ache. The last thing he wanted was to hurt her.

The rest of the morning passed in silence. Everyone knew what had to be done before starting to travel again, and each had their own duties. Right after breakfast, Emile nodded to Fin and him and the three headed to the archery place. Trystian and Gwen would either meet them outside, or

Alaric's Bow: A Book of the Amari

back here if the pack horse was still being loaded.

The wooden overhang gave them the chance to shake some rain off their cloaks before entering the shop. A steady stream of pale smoke rose from the brick chimney, giving Alaric notice that the shop would be warm. A good sign for a bowmaker. Constant damp and cool while shaping the wood would warp it past use.

A small bell rang out as Emile opened the door. A fireplace took up most of one wall, heating the shop effectively. A tall man, blue eyes peering out from beneath shaggy grey eyebrows, watched them enter. Emile leaned against the doorway. Alaric knew the man well enough to see the stance wasn't nearly as relaxed as he looked.

"My friend here," he placed a hand on Fin's shoulder, "wants to take up the bow."

The shop owner looked her up and down. "Don't know that I'd start you off with a longbow like your friend, miss. Recommend something a bit shorter. Get used to the flow of the weapon before you move into something with more punch."

He moved around the workbench, waving a hand over toward a small

Alaric's Bow: A Book of the Amari

assortment of bows leaning against the far wall. The artisan didn't ask questions, simply began to show her various things. In less than an hour, they were back out into the rain. Alaric had the supplies he needed. And Fin was ready to learn what a bow could do.

Trystian and Gwen sat on their horses, waiting. "Get everything?" Trystian asked.

Emile nodded as he mounted his horse. "And Alaric didn't even spend all my gold." Reaching down, he lifted Fin up into the saddle in front of him. "Rain or no rain, we head to Lorien. I've got an appointment to keep."

Alaric touched his heels to his horse's flanks, urging it to follow his companions.

Alaric's Bow: A Book of the Amari

Chapter Eight

The capital looked different than he remembered it. The white stone no longer reflected the afternoon sun. Instead, it was a dull grey, lifeless, and bare of the green vegetation that'd been there six years earlier. Soot from forges blanketed the streets. Kaerdan's war machine was in full swing.

Emile stopped. "Things have changed." His words conveyed the same concern Alaric had. He whispered something in Fin's ear, and she slowly eased out of her customary spot in front of him. "Alaric, Fin's going to ride in with you. If anyone asks, she's your betrothed and her horse went lame."

Nodding, he reached down to help Fin up into his saddle. She settled in against him, making his heart race. "Can I ask why?"

Emile turned back to him, "I'm too old to be marrying her. Trystian wears the token of another. At her age now, she needs to be protected in that way. Your brother's let his army take over the city. If she's not attached, they'd consider her fair bait." He paused. "You've got a nephew, Alaric.

Alaric's Bow: A Book of the Amari

That's why we're in town. To pay homage to the newborn prince." Sarcasm dripped from his voice. "Let me do the talking. We go directly to a place I know that's safe. Only then do we do anything else." He smiled grimly. "I wouldn't go bragging about the relationship if I were you, though."

Emile's warning brought Alaric back to his senses, and the feel of Fin's body next to his became less of a distraction. "Don't worry, Emile. I'll be avoiding the spotlight."

Following the older man, the group made their way toward the city gates. Alaric didn't even try to hear the exchange between the guards. He felt Fin's body tense up as their gaze passed over to her. Thinking swiftly, he placed a quick kiss on the top of her head while meeting their gaze. Satisfied, the guard made notes on a piece of paper while Emile handed the other one some coins. Once the transaction was complete, the guards waved them onward and moved to the next in the line.

Emile led them through the crowded streets. Litter and mud cluttered the drainage lines, causing an overflow into the streets. The paved stones no longer cleaned by anything but the rain. The houses and shops were in varying stages of decay, as well.

Alaric's Bow: A Book of the Amari

This didn't surprise Alaric much. Kaerdan never cared much for how those in the village around their father's castle lived back on the island. He thought Erien would've done more, though. She'd been so caring, so conscientious, back in Antioch. Though there was a good chance that marriage to Kaerdan had changed her. He shoved the thought from his head. That his friend would change her nature that drastically scared him.

By the time Emile stopped them in front of an inn whose owner took pride in its' appearance, Alaric shuddered. He knew things couldn't be good for Erien, and his brother wouldn't see the suffering. But that they allowed the populace of their capital slide into the despair and misery he'd seen shook his very soul.

The inside showed some changes even Alaric didn't expect. The common room was divided by a heavy tapestry, with a large man stationed at the end. "Ladies must go to the right," he intoned as he gestured. "This is a proper establishment. The house ladies will attend to them while you check in this way." His right arm pointed to Alaric's left.

Alaric's Bow: A Book of the Amari

Emile bowed slightly. "We mean no disrespect, good sir, to either the owner or his family. However, I would prefer my daughter and her companion remain with us. This gentleman," he put a hand on Alaric's shoulder, "is her betrothed. I can assure you that nothing improper would occur should we have adjoining rooms."

The large man shook his head. "If they were husband and wife, it would not matter. We follow the rules set down by the new Queen, ones that have consequences if not obeyed."

Gwen put her arms around Fin's slender shoulders. "I will watch over her, Master Amain." She used a name Emile had in the past. One of his many aliases. "Do not fear for her safety." Without another word, the two women disappeared between the hanging swaths of dark silk.

Alaric watched them depart, then looked at Emile for a clue of what to do next. The other man's face seemed relaxed and unconcerned, but his jaw was tight. A brief nod passed between them before heading through the other entrance.

The dark wood tables and chairs gleamed in the warm firelight in the room. Few patrons sat at the tables or bar that

Alaric's Bow: A Book of the Amari

dominated the other side of the room. An older man stopped wiping at the counter. "Master Amain! My friend! It has been too long!" His greeting to Emile seemed genuine, not forced, as he moved around the bar.

"Grendal! Too long, you're right." He embraced the other man.

Laughing, the men broke apart. "What of your daughter, Sera? She is well, I hope?"

"Indeed. She is next door," he gestured to the heavy tapestry splitting the room in half. "But I don't understand. It was never an issue before for us to have adjoining rooms."

"It's the queen, Amain. She and the king—" Grendal spat on the ground, "—they do not get along well. She has enacted certain laws so that women are protected from the likes of his soldiers. If an establishment follows the laws voluntarily, any kingsman who disrupts the women's quarters is dealt with swiftly and severely. But have no fear. I will put you in a room where you can still communicate with her." He clasped Emile's shoulder. "Now, who are your friends?"

Alaric's Bow: A Book of the Amari

Emile smiled, "Tyrone and Alaric. One's good at keeping us safe as we travel, the other is Sera's betrothed. I'll let you figure out which is which." He laughed.

"Welcome, friends. If you travel with Master Amain, you are safe here. Come. Your journey, no doubt, has been a long one. I'm sure you wish for a good rest, better food, and perhaps clean clothes." He grabbed at a set of keys hanging on the wall. "Namine runs the women's side for me. I'm certain Sera and her companion are being well taken care of already. I will take you up to your room and you will be able to know for yourself."

They followed Grendal up the staircase, the older man far more spry than Alaric expected. He stopped before a room at the end of the hall. "This room was set up for instances like yours, Amain. I'm sure you'll feel all is well soon." He handed a key to Emile. "I'll have someone bring up meals in about an hour." The man brushed past Alaric as he headed back down the stairs.

Alaric caught a look on Trystian's face, and looked back at Emile. He moved a single finger to his lips, signaling for silence. Alaric eased a dagger out of the sheath at the small of his back as Trystian

Alaric's Bow: A Book of the Amari

moved toward the door. He didn't know what was on the other side, but Emile's cautious stance made him more than wary. But he knew the man wasn't buying Grendal's reasons.

He watched, his thumb nervously caressing the hilt of his dagger, as Emile waited for Trystian to take up position in front of the door. The older man grasped the doorknob firmly. When Trystian nodded his readiness, Emile twisted the handle and threw the door open in a fluid motion. Alaric followed Trystian as he charged into the room.

"The theatrics weren't necessary, Alaric. I've known you were coming for a week or more now." A female voice called out from a ring of chairs in front of a fireplace.

He stopped. Gwen and Fin sat facing him, their faces a mask. He didn't need the other woman to turn around. He'd recognized Erien's voice the moment she spoke.

Emile broke the silence. "Hello, Your Majesty. To what do we owe this honor?"

She rose, as graceful as Alaric remembered. His heart sank when he saw

Alaric's Bow: A Book of the Amari

the bitterness on her face. The softness replaced with a stony coldness. She'd changed. Or Kaerdan had changed her.

"You can drop the pretense, Emile. I know who you all are. What you are." She didn't even try to disguise the threat. "We can make this easy, or hard. I only need to have a word or three with Kai." Alaric started at her use of his old name. "Alone. Once that discussion is complete, I'll go the way I came in. None need know I was here. Or you were, for that matter."

"And if we don't agree?" Emile had moved closer toward Fin. Alaric knew he'd try to grab her and run. And that Gwen and Trystian would provide cover for their escape.

"It's fine. I agree." Alaric spoke. He locked his gaze with Emile's. "I'm willing to talk. And listen. Provided I have your guarantee my companions will not be harmed or detained in any way while we do."

A tired smile crossed Erien's face. "But of course. You have my word as Queen."

Emile and Fin looked at each other, then the older man nodded once. "I take it the door over there leads to the women's

Alaric's Bow: A Book of the Amari

half of the room?" Alaric watched as Gwen led Fin toward the door. Trystian followed. Emile gave him one last look before he departed and closed the door behind him. Alaric knew he'd be listening in as best he could.

He turned back towards Erien. "What do you—" his question was interrupted as she flew into his arms, kissing him.

For a brief moment, he enjoyed the feel of her lips on his. Her body clung to him. It wasn't right, though. And he knew it. No matter how many times he'd longed for her to come to him when they lived in Antioch, this wasn't right. He broke free of the kiss, only to have her bury her head in his chest, arms locked tight around his waist.

"I've missed you so much," she whispered. "Every night, I go to sleep wishing I could turn back time and run off like you suggested. Honor be damned, I should've listened to you."

"But you didn't, Erien. Is this why you wanted to see me?"

She pulled away slightly, but did not fully let go of him. Raising her head, her eyes locked with his. "I can't leave him. I know that. But give me one night, Kai. One

Alaric's Bow: A Book of the Amari

that I can take with me every time your brother comes to my chamber drunk. A memory I can treasure. Then you and your friends can take your pet and go." Her hand began to pull at his shirt.

Disgusted, he pushed her hand away and grabbed at her wrists. "My name's not Kai. It's Alaric. And Fin is no one's pet." His voice echoed harshly in his own ears.

Confusion ruled Erien's face for a moment. Then, her eyes widened in shock. "You love her."

Alaric let go of her wrists and walked around a chair. Leaning on the back, he exhaled slowly. "It's complicated, Erien."

She laughed, but there wasn't any mirth in it. "You love her, and she doesn't love you. Or you can't gather the courage up to tell her." She sneered at him, "Kaerdan's terrified of you, and you're letting some Amari witch control you. All you would need to do is raise your hand and the entire kingdom could be yours. He's a bully. The people know it. And they're tired of his brutality." She crossed the room toward him. "I'd be yours, as well. Challenge him to a duel and you win me. You win a kingdom. I'd even let you keep that one as a pet if you must. But don't think for a moment you can

Alaric's Bow: A Book of the Amari

turn your back on me and walk away, Kai. You're destined for so much more than some mercenary with a bow."

"I swore an oath, Erien. To keep her safe and out of chains. I'm not going to turn my back on that for any reason." His fingers grasped the chair firmly. "Kai's dead. He and I were on the same boat, yes. But he died. I saw him be buried at sea. Kaerdan has no fear that his half Amari brother is going to show up to challenge his rule." Inhaling deeply, he weighed his next words carefully, knowing they would be the most painful for her to hear. "I'm not sleeping with you, Erien. I'd rather find myself in chains kneeling before your husband than give up Fin."

Shock played across her face, followed by grief. He'd once thought he loved her, yes. A few years ago, he would've jumped at what she offered. But that was then. He'd changed too much.

She was right about something, though. He loved Fin. The idea of betraying her, even if she never looked at him that way, chilled his very soul. Any hope of a relationship with her rested on her choices, her terms. He wasn't about to jeopardize his chances with Fin. She had a very good memory.

Erien's face became a stone mask, unreadable and unyielding. "I give you two days, Alaric." Her voice, defeated, was barely above a whisper. "Conclude your business and quickly. I won't stop him from finding you or your friends."

Without another word, she turned and slid aside a panel of the wall. A man stood there, gold eyes reflecting the torch he carried. "Take me back to the palace," she said.

The Amari stepped aside to allow her to pass, then closed the door behind her. Alaric turned the chair around in one swift motion, falling into it without a thought. His heart raced. Did he just condemn them all to being hunted?

He heard the others come back into the room, but continued to stare into the fire. He wasn't sure if he was numb or overwhelmed knowing that Erien's life was beyond any horror he might have imagined. Kaerdan sober was bad enough. Drunk would've been even uglier.

"We have two days. I say we leave in one." Emile's voice pierced the fog in his

Alaric's Bow: A Book of the Amari

head. "Fin and I will do what we must tonight. We leave again at first light."

At some point, Gwen handed him a plate with food on it. "Eat," she commanded. "Emile's going to move us fast for a few days. He'll want to get us out of Lorien lands sooner rather than later."

"Shouldn't worry yourself too much about your lady friend, Alaric," Trystian's voice stayed low. "She's a survivor. If she couldn't handle her life, she would've been dead by now." Alaric heard the scrape of a whetstone across the large man's blade. "You did good, turning her down. She'd have sunk her claws in deep and had you leading a rebellion if you'd slept with her."

"What is so important that Emile and Fin had to come back here?" Alaric asked, not really expecting an answer.

"Twenty years ago, he found Fin. In a sewer here in Lorien. She was really young, maybe five years old, and thought she could hide. Barely knew how to keep her eyes hidden. Before he took her out, he left a message down there. Promising to come back with her every ten years. So her family would know when they could find her again, or any other unchained Amari knew when help would be there."

Alaric's Bow: A Book of the Amari

Alaric switched his chair around, facing Trystian. The other man sat calmly on a sofa, sharpening his blade with even strokes.

"Have her parents ever come? Or another Amari?"

Trystian shrugged, "No. I hadn't been with them long when we came back the first time. Fin was still fairly young then. Hadn't learned to guard her emotions like she can now. Tore her up to leave without anyone. Not even a sigil left behind saying her parents had even gone down there."

"She changed not long after that," Gwen spoke up. "Stopped hoping, began to see us as her family. If anyone was there tonight, I think she'd be cautious before accepting their word as truth. We've had too many close calls. She's seen how easily other Amari fall prey to slavers who pretend to be something they're not."

The sound of the secret door opening up alerted them all. Trystian and Gwen took up a ready stance while Alaric grabbed at his bow. If he could string it fast enough, he might get a shot in.

A woman stepped into the room, her head lowered. Short brown hair and a slight frame. A thin band of metal encircled her wrist.

"Holly?" Alaric said, stunned.

She raised his head. "My mistress sends word. She has been summoned by His Majesty, to answer for her whereabouts earlier today. She regrets to inform you she may not be able to give you the full time promised." Silently, Holly retreated back through the hidden passage.

Alaric looked at Trystian and Gwen. "Gwen, grab their packs. We'll meet them at the exit," Trystian's beard shook as he spoke. "Alaric, keep that bow strung. We may need it yet."

Within minutes, the trio had everything in hand. "There's a back staircase. Emile used it to go out with Fin." Gwen motioned to them from the connecting door. "We should be fine using it. He wouldn't have taken her that way if it wasn't safe."

Alaric shrugged, adjusting his pack on his shoulders. "Go. I'll take up the rear." With Gwen leading the way, the three of them made their way down the staircase quickly.

Trystian moved to the front, easing the door to the alleyway open. Peering

Alaric's Bow: A Book of the Amari

outside, he motioned for them to follow. Alaric glanced behind once, making sure no one followed them.

The passage was narrow and dark. Rats chittered amongst the trash as they passed through. "Gwen," Trystian whispered, "we don't have time to get the horses. Leave them. Head to the stables, grab the larger packs with the tents. Meet us at the exit."

Gwen nodded once, then disappeared down a small passage. A sliver of a moon gave a little light as Alaric followed Trystian through a maze of back streets. He knew they were being hunted.

As they turned a corner, the castle on top of the city came into view. Alaric paused, his feet moving almost involuntarily toward the bright light burning from a single window of the complex. Erien was up there, with Kaerdan. And his brother most likely wasn't being kind.

"Your friend's either talking by now, or in a world of pain. She gave us the chance to escape. Honor her sacrifice by taking it." Trystian's gruff voice echoed in his ear.

Shaking off the feeling, Alaric turned his back on the path leading to the keep. In his heart, he closed the door that led to Erien at the same time.

Soldiers were beginning to search for them now. They kept to shadows and back alleys, moving in bursts of speed. Alaric's mind filled with thoughts of Fin. He and Trystian had to get there unseen. If they didn't, if they were followed…

"Keep your mind on the task at hand, Islander." Trystian growled at him as his large arm flattened Alaric against a wall. "If it's a choice between you and Fin, you know who I'll save."

A small patrol, maybe four or five troops, jogged past the alley where they hid. Alaric had almost stepped in front of them. Trystian was right. He shook his head, clearing away the worry and concern. Fin's safety was what mattered, not what might happen to him. "Sorry," he muttered.

After several blocks, they came to a dark courtyard. The paving stones beneath his feet became slick with muck. Three exposed pipes jutted out of walls, sewage and waste overtaking the bottom quarter of each tube. Trystian leaned against one wall and motioned Alaric to take up a position on the opposite side of the courtyard. Anyone

Alaric's Bow: A Book of the Amari

coming out of those pipes would now either meet Trystian's sword or Alaric's bow.

He kept an eye on the alley they'd come down. It bent between the street and their location, so he didn't have a clear light of sight. Instead, he willed his heart to slow down and listened for any sound beyond the rats running about.

A whistled note pierced the quiet. Trystian answered in kind. Alaric lowered his bow as Gwen emerged from the dark.

"Not out yet?" she whispered.

Trystian shook his head, then jutted his chin to the point on the wall he wanted her to take up. "It's early yet. They don't know what's going on. We wait."

For the next hour, they stood. Not speaking. Listening and waiting. Alaric's legs didn't bother him. Not yet. But he knew the muscles in his back weren't going to be happy when they finally stopped running.

His body was still, but his mind raced. He knew he'd not hesitate to surrender himself if that's what it took to get Fin out safely. Then again, he couldn't trust any promise Kaerdan might make. The minute his brother knew about Fin, she would become a weapon to be used against Alaric. He'd need to make sure she got out

Alaric's Bow: A Book of the Amari

of town first. If he was lucky, he'd be able to go with her.

"Stop that thought, Alaric." Gwen's voice drifted to him. "Only way we get out of here is if we all do."

A rustling came from one of the pipes. Alaric's hand flew to his quiver, drawing out an arrow. It was notched and ready to fly before Emile emerged.

"She's right, Alaric. If we have to go, we all go," the older man commented as he climbed free of the pipe. Gwen knelt down and reached her arm in, helping pull Fin free of the small space. "If you three are here, it means we leave tonight." Emile didn't even wait for an explanation. He went over to the pile of packs Gwen had deposited on the ground. Rummaging through the stack, he tossed one over to Fin. "We head north. Caerlynn's got a new ruler. Rumor has it he's allowing the Amari to live normal lives."

"Met someone this time?" Trystian kept his voice low.

"No, but someone had left word." Emile shouldered his pack and one of the tents. "There's a way out of the city, but it'll be tricky. Stay close." He slid down the other alleyway, not looking back.

Alaric's Bow: A Book of the Amari

Alaric waited for the others to follow and took up the rear. Fin and Emile both were covered in sludge from the sewer, but moved quickly.

Emile led them through a few more side streets, deftly avoiding patrols and drunks. Finally, he stopped them at the back door of a house. Laughter, punctuated by screaming, poured from the open windows. His mind rebelled against what was probably going on inside.

"Gwen, Fin, keep your heads down. If anyone asks, you belong to us. Don't speak, just point to one of us. Women aren't expected to speak in this house unless given permission by whoever paid for them that night." Emile looked at Alaric. "You'll need to act like you own one of them. Don't let what you'll see get under your skin. If they even suspect you're half Amari, they'll put you under the same rules they would Fin or Gwen. We won't be in here long. I hope." He turned and knocked once.

The door opened. Bright candlelight made the person in the doorway barely recognizable. His bulk, however, wasn't as easy to hide. "Full up tonight if you're buying. Or are you selling?"

Alaric's Bow: A Book of the Amari

"Neither. I need to see Paul." Emile spoke.

The doorman squinted, trying to make them out. "No one sees Paul unless he knows they're coming. And he didn't tell me you were expected."

Emile rummaged about in his tunic, pulling a small item out of a hidden pocket. Alaric couldn't tell what it was. "Give him this," he put it in the bouncer's hand. "If he still won't see us, I'll be surprised."

The large man stared at the item in his hand. "I know what it is. He'll want to see you." He pointed at Gwen and Fin. "Keep the wenches under control. If they're mistaken for workers, we aren't held responsible for damages." He turned around and gestured at them to follow him.

The main room was filled with men and a few women. Most of the women wore little except for the metal band around their necks. A few of the men were in the same condition. For a pleasure house, it was relatively clean. From the screams coming from above them, that's where most of the business was conducted.

Their guide stopped on the other side of the room before an iron bound door.

Alaric's Bow: A Book of the Amari

"Wait here," he intoned, then lifted the bar and went inside.

"How come they're hiding the red-haired one?" A drunk voice bellowed from across the room.

Alaric moved between the man staggering toward Fin. "Because she's already paid for."

The man swayed on his feet, inches away from Alaric's face. Sweat poured down his ruddy cheeks, the odor combining with the ale to make him truly reek. "Ain't no Amari whore that can't be paid for more than once. What's your price?"

Without thinking, Alaric drew his dagger and put it under the drunk's chin. "She's no Amari, you fool. No chain on her, no gold eyes. And I paid dearly for first rights. You won't see enough coin in your entire life to come close to having enough." He shoved the drunk away from them.

He lost his footing, falling flat on the floor. The man's eyes narrowed, "Watch what you do, boy. I ain't afraid of you. If I want something, I get it. You can get some coin out of it, or not."

Another man stepped in front of Alaric, a quarterstaff at the ready. "Not in my house, Damien. This man's paid for her,

Alaric's Bow: A Book of the Amari

she's his. Get your drunk ass out of here. And take your crew with you. Not taking your money tonight."

The other man rose, shooting a hate-filled glance at Alaric. He pulled two other men away from the women they were fondling and headed to the exit.

"Sorry, Emile. Sometimes Damien forgets his manners around here." He pointed his staff towards the open door. "This way. Let's get you on the road before anyone else gets stupid."

Alaric followed down a passageway. The bouncer nodded once when he passed through the open door, then closed it behind him. He heard the heavy bar being placed back over the door.

"I don't like coming here, Paul. But the need was urgent tonight."

"I understand, my friend. Rumor runs rampant. Half my clientele for the night went in search of your archer friend there. And the unchained Amari." The man with the quarterstaff responded. "I owe you quite a bit. I daresay we might be even after tonight."

Emile chuckled, "Oh, probably. That drunk's not going to cause you problems later on, is he?"

Alaric's Bow: A Book of the Amari

"Damien? Nah. He and his crew like to pretend they can spot an Amari by sight. They're wrong more than they're right. Militia knows that. Even if he went to them right now and said he knew where your group was at, they wouldn't believe him." Paul stopped under a torch, giving Alaric his first real look at the man.

Slightly built and closely cropped blonde hair, he was fairly unremarkable. But his hands grasped the weapon in such a way that Alaric knew he'd be dangerous in a fight.

"You know the way from here, right?" Paul asked Emile. "I need to get back. Need to keep things moving smoothly."

Emile nodded. "Thanks, my friend. I won't be back this way again."

Paul brushed past the group and headed back toward the common area.

Emile worked aside one brick in the wall, revealing a small opening. He reached inside. The wall in front of them began to move, a small shower of dirt falling as it shifted.

"We go out this way," Emile stated as he lifted the torch out of the ring on the wall. "Keep close. The ground's uneven.

Alaric's Bow: A Book of the Amari

When we get the door closed, we'll find another torch to give us a little more light."

"How far is it?" Fin asked.

"Far enough that we'll spend at least one night in here. And be at the edge of Kaerdan's reach when we come out." The man waved them on to pass through the portal.

Alaric ducked through the opening, not wanting to go far into the enveloping dark. The musty aroma of earth surrounded him.

Emile pushed down on a lever sticking out of the stone near the door, and it slid back into place.

"Now what, Emile?" Fin spoke from near Alaric. The darkness was so deep he'd not realized how close she was.

"We get another torch lit, and walk. There's a pool of fresh water up ahead. We can camp there for tonight. Rest. Get cleaned up. No one's going to bother us in here."

Gwen's face brightened as the torch in her hand caught some of the flame from Emile's. She passed it on to Alaric. "One in the front, one in the back. Let's move."

Slowly, they made their way through the darkness. He didn't know how long they'd be in the dark, but swore he'd get Fin practicing with her bow once they were above ground again.

He lost track of time. The only thing keeping him from going mad was the flickering torch he held, matched by the one Emile held up ahead of him. The meager light kept whatever might be hiding in the dark at bay.

Alaric never had issues with the dark before the scorpion sting. Since then, though, things had changed slightly. His encounter with the total blackness of death changed him. He knew what was out there, waiting for him. He'd escaped death once, thanks to Fin. And now it waited for the chance to strike again.

Emile stopped, his torch no longer moving as he did. As Alaric approached, the walls opened up around him. The cavern's walls, decorated with veins of quartz, reflected the torchlight. A small river flowed through one side. Clear water collected in a small pool in the center before disappearing through another opening. "We stop here for the night," Emile stated. "We can fill up our water skins, clean up in the pool. Get some sleep."

Alaric's Bow: A Book of the Amari

No one needed to be told anything else. The routine of setting up camp began. Bedrolls came out, but not the tents. Trystian got a fire started and rummaged about for ingredients for that night's dinner. Gwen and Fin went to the far side of the pond to fill up water stores and bathe. Alaric resisted the urge to watch. The light wasn't enough where he'd see anything, but felt they should still have some privacy. The splash, followed immediately by a shocked squeal, made him turn his head though.

Fin was standing waist deep in the water. Her hands pushed water from her hair, giving him a tantalizing view of her naked profile. The shadows kept details hidden, but not enough to keep his loins from tightening at the sight. "No peeking, Islander," Trystian whispered from the fire. "Best not let either of them know you saw anything. They're strong women. Stronger than most. And Fin's just as likely to castrate you as anything. They make the choices, not us."

Alaric turned away and moved closer to the fire. Trystian was right. Any relationship he might have with Fin would be because she chose it.

Alaric's Bow: A Book of the Amari

Chapter Nine

The light ahead grew larger as they approached. But also fainter. Emile had warned them they'd reach the end of the tunnel today, but wouldn't be able to leave it. That would wait for dawn. When they could emerge without giving away the location and still have a full day to travel.

"We keep watch tonight, no fires." Emile extinguished his torch and motioned at Alaric to do the same. "Few know of this route, and it must be kept that way."

Alaric took a wistful look at the rapidly fading light. The smell of fresh air teased his nose. That was something, at least. One more night and he'd be out under the open sky again.

They moved quickly, before it became too dark to see. No sense to do much beyond pass around some bread or dried beef. Alaric found a section of the wall that wasn't too rocky and settled in to sleep.

Someone or something nudged his foot, rousing him. Emile stood over him. "Your turn," he whispered. Alaric rose, taking in what little he could see. The moon was full, giving them a faint light. Trystian

Alaric's Bow: A Book of the Amari

slept, his sword in his hand. Gwen and Emile both grabbed at blankets, ready to rest. Fin silently folded hers before tying it to her pack.

Alaric walked toward her, avoiding both his sleeping companions and their gear. "I don't think we'll be shooting tonight," he said, keeping his voice light.

Fin snorted, "You think?" she replied sarcastically. "Trying to be funny, Islander?"

Her tone stung. "Not really, Fin. Just making conversation."

She scrambled up on a rock close enough to the exit to observe, but not be seen. "It's not you, Alaric. It's this tunnel. The darkness. I hate it."

He took up a position opposite of her. "I understand that. It's oppressive in a lot of ways. I've felt like death was waiting for me since we first came in here. But I've had issues with darkness ever since that damn scorpion bit me."

"That's natural, I suppose. At least you know where your fear comes from. That's half way to conquering it. I don't know." She plucked a small patch of moss off of the wall next to her, picking it to pieces as she spoke. "I've been in this tunnel

Alaric's Bow: A Book of the Amari

before. The sewers where Emile found me were dark, but I was more afraid then of the light. Because that meant someone was coming to chain me, make me their pet. The dark was a good thing."

"So, what's changed?"

Fin threw the remains of the moss towards the sheltered opening. It bounced against the bushes blocking the way out, finally coming to rest on a rather nasty looking thorn. "Maybe it's me that's changed. Maybe I'm tired of hiding, being on alert all the time. Never able to relax." She let out a heavy sigh. "I've been hiding for over twenty years, Alaric. No one should have to do that just to stay free."

A single tear wove a path down her face, catching the moonlight. Alaric rose, crossing the small space to be closer to her. "So, stop hiding. When it's just the five of us. You can relax. We won't treat you any differently, won't put a leash on you," he whispered. His heart broke to hear her vocalize her pain. Even though he was living a life hidden himself, it wasn't to her extent. He didn't have to hide his eyes just to stay alive.

She didn't reply, and wouldn't look at him. Her head turned toward the

Alaric's Bow: A Book of the Amari

brambles. Alaric moved back to his spot on the opposite side. And kept the watch in silence.

Three hours later, when the light began to shift, Fin spoke again. "It's time. Let's wake the others and get moving."

Alaric nodded, easing his way off the small ledge he'd perched on. While Fin got the rest up, he shouldered his pack and adjusted the quiver on his hip. He preferred to keep the bow unstrung, but decided to have it ready just in case. There was no way of knowing what they'd encounter when they left.

He did a quick survey of the area once Emile moved toward the exit, making sure nothing was left behind. As he turned back around, Fin was there. Her green eyes gold for the first time in weeks. She stretched up, planting a gentle kiss on his cheek. "Thank you," she whispered.

He smiled, resisting the urge to pull her into him. "What did I do right?"

"You listened." With those words, her eyes reverted back to the green she let the world see. The mask back in place, she followed the others out of the cave.

Still smiling, Alaric followed. Tonight, he'd have to find the carcass of an

Alaric's Bow: A Book of the Amari

animal if he could. Teach her the difference between hitting trees and flesh with her arrows. And maybe she'd allow him into her world a little bit more.

Alaric's Bow: A Book of the Amari

About the Author

Born in the late 60's, KateMarie has lived most of her life in the Pacific NW. While she's always been creative, she didn't turn towards writing until 2008. She found a love for the craft. With the encouragement of her husband and two children, she started submitting her work to publishers. When she's not taking care of her family, KateMarie enjoys attending events for the Society for Creative Anachronism. The SCA has allowed her to combine both a creative nature and love of history. She currently resides with her family and two cats in what she likes to refer to as "Seattle Suburbia".

You can find KateMarie at the following sites:

Twitter: @DaughterHauk
FaceBook: http://www.facebook.com/pages/KateMarie-Collins/217255151699492
Her blog: http://www.katemariecollins.wordpress.com

Alaric's Bow: A Book of the Amari

Alaric's Bow: A Book of the Amari

Other Solstice Shadows titles By KateMarie Collins

Fin's Magic: A Book of the Amari

Fin depends on her companions to keep her safe…and out of chains. As one of the Amari, the only race that can harness magic, she longs for a normal life. One where she didn't have to constantly look over her shoulder, and she could fall in love.

Alaric fell hard for Fin from the moment he laid his eyes on her three years ago. He swore an oath to keep her safe, even if it meant his life. But he knew that any relationship he could hope to have with her would be on her terms.

When a king offers them the chance at a normal life, Fin's cautious. And rightly so, as there are others who think she's the one to lead the Amari from a life of slavery.

Arine's Sanctuary

The Moreja Sisterhood exists to rescue boys from abuse and arranged marriages. Arine's on assignment, bringing Cavon back

Alaric's Bow: A Book of the Amari

to her home in Sanctuary, when she discovers something terrifying.

He can do magic.

When the chance comes up for her to go back out and rescue her own brother, sold off by her mother ten years earlier, Arine eagerly takes the chance. But can she talk him into coming home to Sanctuary with her? And can they get there before the Domine's army, bent on controlling the magic?

Alaric's Bow: A Book of the Amari

Daughter of Hauk
Book 1 of The Raven Chronicles

What would you do, if you found out your life was a lie?

After you were dead?

Arwenna Shalian spent her life in loyal service to a God she was never meant to serve. Tricked by her fellow priests, she betrayed a man she thought she loved by binding a demon to him. One that would send him to the brink of madness.

Can she find a way to forgive herself? And what of Hauk, the God she was Marked to serve? Will He find her and give her the chance to undo what she's done, or leave her at the mercy of the creatures that torture her soul?

Son of Corse
Book 2 of The Raven Chronicles

It's been almost two years since Arwenna banished the Demon Corse from her world. Life has been good. Idyllic, almost.

The illusion is shattered in a heartbeat during her sister's wedding. Not only are once-dead enemies back, but they've stolen Arwenna's only child, Sera.

Alaric's Bow: A Book of the Amari

The price Arwenna will have to pay to save her daughter is high. Can she muster the strength to make a pact that jeopardizes not just her own soul, but that of an entire world?

Alaric's Bow: A Book of the Amari

Mark of the Successor

Dominated and controlled by an abusive mother, Lily does what she can to enjoy fleeting moments of normality. When a break from school only provides the opportunity for more abuse at home, the sudden appearance of a stranger turns her world even bleaker. Disappearing without a trace, he has left a lingering fear in Lily. His parting words to her mother, "Have her ready to travel tomorrow," is something her mind refuses to accept.

Running away is the only answer. But before Lily can execute her plan, a shimmering portal appears in her room. Along with two strangers who promise to help keep her safe. With time running out, she accepts their offer for escape and accompanies them into a brand new world. A world in which she is the kidnapped daughter of a Queen, and the heir to the throne of Tiadar.

Can she find her own strength to overcome both an abusive past and avoid those who would use her as a means to power?

Made in the USA
Columbia, SC
19 March 2019